CW01661470

Soul-wise

with love
from
Helen +
Robert
xxx

Soul-wise

Excerpts from talks given by

Radhanath Swami

Tulsi Books

Published and printed by:

Tulsi books
(A division of Sri Tulsi Trust)
7, K.M. Munshi marg,
Girgaum Chowpatty,
Mumbai - 400007
www.tulsibooks.com

This book is dedicated to
His Divine Grace A.C. Bhaktivedanta Swami Prabhupada.

ISBN : 978-81-910355-1-3

INTRODUCTION

To seek is the nature of the living force. The search of the soul seems never-ending. But the real need is not just to seek, but to seek the right thing from the right source.

Wisdom is the quality of having experience, knowledge and good judgment about the truths of life. Essentially, knowledge that not just informs but also actually transforms is called wisdom. Just like a diamond is nothing but an ordinary piece of coal, which, with the help of nature's wisdom, has transformed into the most precious jewel. Similarly, the soul with the help of the right knowledge from the right source has the potential of being transformed into Soul-wise.

When the sun shines on a snow-capped mountain, the layers of snow melt down helplessly. Similarly, when the sun-like wisdom shines on a covered entity, layers of ignorance start melting away, thus uncovering a Soul-wise.

Real learning has to be holistic and not just in one dimension. When learning happens using multiple faculties, the depth of its influence is always greater. This book is a filled with diverse wisdom articles which will make us ponder, wonder and help us overcome the blunder of ignorance which leads to suffering and sorrow.

This book is a collection of pearls of wisdom, in the necklace of life, for the beauty of the soul.

We hope that the reader will be benefited by the articles in this book and will find them applicable in various situations in life.

Contents

From Nature 57

Irony of This World 77

Values to Strive For

Love Gives, Greed Takes

Education and knowledge should never be used to simply fulfill our greed. When people use the knowledge they acquire to satisfy their greed, the society ends up being in a big mess. Is this what we want?

Our consciousness by nature is eternal, full of knowledge and full of joy. In a real joyful state based on truth, there can be no greed. Real joy and love wants only to be shared with everyone else. The nature of love is to give; the nature of greed is to take.

Real pleasure is in giving the love of our hearts. That love already exists in our hearts. But our consciousness is impure. We are not aware of who we are. Through the process of purification, our consciousness becomes clear and transparent. Through such transparent consciousness, we can experience God at every moment. And when we perceive God at every moment, we realize, not feel or believe or think, but realize that, whether someone calls God Allah or Jehovah or Krishna or Rama or Buddha, there is only one God, who is the supreme object of love and the source of all that exists.

A Grateful Heart

All of us can find real liberation, real satisfaction in this life and beyond. And that is why there are so many spiritual systems within this world. Religion comes from the Greek word religio, which means "to bind back." Yoga is a Sanskrit word, which means to reunite. It's the same word, same essence. Why is there so much fighting? Because people are more concerned with the superficialities of religion than they are with actually developing the real characteristics of devotion and integrity towards truth. Through prayer, meditation, and various spiritual practices, we can reconnect with our own essence. Spirituality is meant to awaken the eternal potential to love and to be an instrument of that love in our life. By reconnecting with our own essence and by accessing that empowerment, we can be instruments of positive change in our world.

Gratitude is an essential quality to access the empowerment of God. Our heart is like a field, all our good qualities are like the seed. Our morality, integrity, spiritual practices, prayers and meditation are meant for watering the seed. But the fertility of the soil of our heart is our humility and our gratitude.

Without being grateful, we can't really receive. Real culture is based on the principle of gratitude. A person can be happy in any situation if he is grateful, but a person can never be happy in any situation unless he is grateful. But we should be as grateful for our failures as for our successes. We should be grateful for the dishonor that we receive as well as for the honor. Because of that gratitude, we are grateful for the opportunity to grow and to learn from that experience. And therefore we do learn and grow from that experience. Gratitude is the foundational principle for all spiritual growth and it's the foundation for basic human kindness.

Compassion–the highest spiritual truth

The fundamental need for all of us is love. Every living being is looking for pleasure—from the insignificant insect to the kings and prime ministers. Every one is seeking pleasure, but there is only one pleasure that can reach the heart, that is the pleasure of experiencing the heart's need to love and to receive love. The pleasures of sensual experience, fame, acquisition of wealth, etc. can reach the mind and the senses, but they don't really touch the heart. What if you were the proprietor of everything on earth when you were the only being on earth? There will be no one to love you and there will be no one to be loved by you. We need love, that's our nature.

One thing that every spiritual path has in common is the characteristic of compassion. One who actually follows a spiritual path is an instrument of compassion. In Buddhism, one of the cardinal principles Lord Buddha taught is ahimsa, which means non-violence, respecting the integrity of the life, liberty and pursuit of happiness of all living beings, regardless of their race, religion, sects, economic or educational backgrounds or even their species—to be compassionate towards others. In the Jain religion, they are very strict vegetarians because they want to reduce the amount of violence that they commit to others. During my spiritual search, while I was traveling in Iran, I studied Islam during the month of Ramadan from a very wonderful scholar of Koran. He told me that they follow the fast of Ramadan to develop compassion. He explained that people are hungry because they don't have what they need. Giving charity to them to get the tax laid off is good, but it is not really fulfilling to the heart.

To give in charity to get your name exalted is good, but it doesn't touch your heart. But to give in charity because you actually feel for the suffering of someone else and out of love you really want to help that person, that is real charity. He fasted so that he could know what the pains of hunger are like and when we he sees someone hungry, he feels compassion for that person. The highest and most pleasing service that one can offer is to be willing to accept inconvenience and difficulty in order to show care and compassion to another.

The Balancing Act

To balance our lives is a very important part of spirituality. We have our occupation and we should be as effective as possible in our performance. We may have a family, but what are the actual needs of a family? Loyalty, care and affection. We see people who become very successful on one level, but are always in anxiety because of their dysfunctional family. Charity begins at home. We must invest time and energy not only into our business, but also into our family and our spiritual needs, through morality, integrity and spiritual practice.

Perfect Charity

Charity is of three types: charity for the body, charity for the mind and charity for the soul.

To give food, shelter, clothes and hospitalization is charity for the body. To encourage people to be good to others and to be friendly is charity for the mind. To give transcendental knowledge and facilities for people to be educated in spiritual life is charity for the soul. All three must go together side by side.

From a spiritual point of view, today even many rich people are more poverty stricken than the poor. We should definitely help the poor by giving what they need to maintain their bodies. But we should not neglect the rich either. They are suffering too.

80% of the people in the upper income bracket have to take sleeping pills to fall asleep. What does that mean? They have so much money and prestige. They have beautiful houses, Mercedes cars, silken clothes, water beds, all kinds of guards and security devices around their homes, and yet they are so miserable and ridden with anxiety that they cannot even sleep. Yet in Mumbai, I see people just sleeping right on the bare street. They do not take sleeping pills; in fact they sleep within seconds. So who is happier? Who has more peace of mind in life? All sectors of society—whether rich or poor—are in need of the charity of transcendental knowledge.

Finding Contentment

People are discontent. Because of this discontent, there is no peace in the world. The scientists and the technologists are thinking, "If we can make a very luxurious type of lifestyle, everyone will be content." So we have luxurious skyscrapers, but many times people are jumping off them to commit suicide. We have big airplanes, but we also terrorists putting bombs in them. We have rocket ships and they are exploding in mid air. We spend billions of dollars of taxpayer's money. For what? For some contentment and peace in life. Who has found it? Is there even one person who can say "Yes, I'm very happy." Perhaps we may find one. But examine him the next day when circumstances change and he loses those very things that bring him happiness. What then? Things in this world change.

We are not against modern technology. We are against the mentality of greed and discontent that is motivating it.

Human life is meant for the ultimate pleasure, the ultimate contentment and the ultimate realization of the love of God. Without self-realization, a human being is miserable and unfortunate.

Unconditional Service

One of the most famous inaugural presidential addresses in the United States history was given by John Fitzgerald Kennedy. He said, "Ask not what your country can do for you, ask what you can do for your country." People stood up and he got applause that lasted for a long time, and it echoes even today, fifty years later. People's hearts are very deeply affected by unconditional service, even on the material platform. But when that unconditional service is on the spiritual platform with consciousness of God, the all-attractive Supreme, that unconditional service attracts even God, leave alone the other living entities in this world.

Strength of Humility

To achieve anything in this world is a struggle. A bird in order to fly in the air has to beat its wings. In order to continue to fly, it has to continuously beat its wings. A swimmer in order to swim in the river has to continuously beat his hands and feet. The moment the bird stops beating its wings, it begins to fall. The moment the swimmer stops beating his legs, he begins to drown. Struggle is a part of life.

Similarly, the law of nature in this world is to make one proud and to infatuate the ego. Even a pauper is proud of his penny. Rich people are decorating themselves with better diamond jewelery than other rich people, and the poor are sleeping over better rags than other poor people. Almost everyone is competing against peers to get a more prestigious position. Almost everyone wants honor and respect. It is the nature of illusion to pull our consciousness down to the egoistic platform. But our goal is different.

We have to struggle against the tendency of egoism and exploitation, and we have to take the position of being humble; not to exploit but to serve, not to seek respect, but to give respect. If we just try our best, God will give us the power to succeed. Then we can experience the highest treasure of true spiritual humility. In that humility, we can understand the greatness and glory of the Supreme Lord, which brings us the ultimate bliss.

Determination Attracts Higher Powers

There was once a sparrow who laid her eggs on a beach. In her absence the ocean stole the eggs away. Not finding her eggs on return, she threatened the ocean to return the eggs back. Seeing no response from the ocean the sparrow vowed to dry up the ocean.

Obviously, the ocean didn't take the sparrow's threat seriously. Firm to achieve her goal, she began taking one drop of water at a time in her tiny beak and carrying it to a distant place. Determined against all odds she continued, and it was her determination that attracted a higher power—the power of the king of all birds, Garuda, the mighty eagle bird carrier of Lord Vishnu. Garuda ordered the ocean to return her eggs, and, being fearful of the mighty bird, the ocean did so.

Our God consciousness—humility, devotion and love of God—are like the eggs that have drowned in the huge ocean of our pride, egoism and spiritual lethargy. Like the mother sparrow, we have no hope of getting rid of them. But if with the determination of that little bird, we decide, "I am going to do it no matter what," then God will take the job upon Himself. He will deliver our souls from this ocean of ignorance, pride, egoism and laziness.

Humility Means Honesty

Humility really means honesty. Humility simply means being truthful. What do we have to brag about? If God does not make the sun rise, what would you do? Did you create your brain? Did you create your eyes to see? Did you create your heart to beat? Did you create your arms to act? As they say in British parlance, "Do not be proud of borrowed plumes." Whatever we have is not ours. We have the free will to use what God gives us in a good way or in an evil way or in a spiritual way. We have that free will and, according to what we do and what we say, the karma is going to come back on us. But still all the facilities we have are coming from a power way beyond our own. Even if you are young and strong now, but by the power of time, how long will you remain young and strong? The body is under the control of nature, the mind is under the control of nature. So humility really means to be honest.

nityo nityanam chetanas chetananam
eko bahunam yo vidadhati kaman
(Katha Upanisad 2.2.13)

The above verse explains that there is one supreme eternal and all others are subordinate to that one supreme eternal. So the fact is that we are always subordinate to the supreme.

Hitler was subordinate to the supreme. The Lord gave him a mind and a body and he totally misused it and exploited it. He tortured and killed others and accumulated oceans and oceans, mountains and mountains of horrible karma upon himself, but ultimately he is dead and gone and his soul has to go to the next place to get his karma.

Alexander, the great, came and conquered so many parts of the world, but where is he now? He was conquered by time. So everyone is subordinate to the power of God. So to be humble means to be realistic and honest. To be proud is to be simply dishonest, ungrateful and unrealistic. To be proud is an illusion. Of course in the world today to be proud is a very cool situation. People like proud people, but the fact is that pride is an illusion and it is a miserable condition for the heart. Humility means to have enough integrity to be honest with the reality of our life before God.

The Greatest Charity

We should be good, charitable and pious. But we should also know the best charity for the human form of life. There is charity for the body, the mind and the soul. You can feed the hungry man and it is a good thing. But that person whom you feed is going to be hungry again. If you can teach a person how to be enlightened in devotional consciousness and revive his or her original spiritual consciousness, that person will never have to be hungry again. That person has achieved a step beyond. That is the greatest charity. Why not utilize our human birth for the greatest thing available?

The scriptures explain that one of the foremost duties of a family person is to give in charity. When we have something, we should be willing to share it with those who are in need. And if we don't share what we have, we become hard-hearted. The greatest charity you can give is an excellent example for others to follow.

Penetrating the Cloud of False Ego

False ego is the basic principle of all material bondage. It is the beginning and the end of material entanglement. The beginning of all our sufferings in this world is when we think "I am the doer; I am the enjoyer and I am very good. Just see what I have done; just see who I am."

From the insignificant insect to the blade of grass, all are covered by the false ego. A fully conscious spiritual entity has an eternal relationship with God in the spiritual world. Such an entity knows the truth, knows God and is full of all wisdom and bliss. However, when under illusion, that same soul thinks, "I am this blade of grass, I don't think; I don't act; I simply stand here, doing nothing." This is the power of the cloud of the false ego.

The only purpose of human life is to penetrate the cloud of false ego, enter into the light of the spiritual sky and to revive our eternal relationship with God. Cultivating humility means fighting against this principle of false ego.

In Giving We Receive

If you do not feel loved, it is probably because you are not showing love. If you do not feel respect, it is probably because you are not showing respect.

Human nature is that people reciprocate with what you give them. If you are impersonal to others, most people will be impersonal to you. If you do not show care and affection for others, people will probably ignore you. That is human nature.

So anyone can say, "Nobody loves me. Everybody is so impersonal to me." But I have seldom found someone who extends himself to be caring, loving and affectionate towards others and doesn't receive love from others. How you behave with others draws certain qualities from within them. If you insult others, you draw out their anger. If you praise others, you draw out their pride. If you are affectionate to others, you can draw out whatever affection is within their hearts. In giving, we receive.

Love means to give

The essential need within every living being is to seek pleasure. What do people do for pleasure? Now, different types of living entities have different standards of pleasure and they work in different ways to achieve them. For a little ant, the pleasure is a grain of sugar. For a moth, its pleasure is light. And we've seen what they'll do to attain that grain of sugar, how hard they will work to achieve that light, even taking the risk of their lives. For some people, their pleasure is to satisfy their ego by inflicting pain and harm on others. Some people find pleasure in being famous, in being adored and aggrandized. Some find pleasure in being worshiped, while some others find pleasure in acquisition of wealth, acquisition of property, acquisition of the power that comes with all these things. A mother finds pleasure in giving satisfaction to her child. A father finds pleasure in seeing the family prosper.

Everyone is looking for pleasure. That essential need for pleasure, in its most important form, is the pleasure of love. Even if you were the proprietor of everything on the entire planet earth but you were the only person on earth, you would be unhappy. There can be no real satisfaction of the heart without having people to love and without being loved. The real problem in the world is poverty of the heart. The only way to fill that hunger is love. The only thing that touches the heart is love. To love means to give.

The child gives nothing to the mother, but the mother is found to take more satisfaction in that child than practically anything or anyone else and all she is doing is giving her love, all she is doing is just sacrificing. Because that is real pleasure. Love is not just to take, love is to give. The more you give, the more genuine your giving is, the more people will naturally reciprocate, thus bringing satisfaction to the heart.

The Spirit is Me

The Real You

Can you see a thought? Touch it or taste it? None of the senses can witness a thought. It can be witnessed only by the mind. A thought is an expression of the mind.

What is the nature of the mind? The mind is linked to the senses. The senses perceive an object and relay the gathered information to the mind. The mind responds to that object by saying, "I like it" or "I do not like it", "I want it" or "I do not want it." The mind is accepting or rejecting, hankering for its wants or lamenting for its losses. This is the function of the mind: simply to perceive things through the senses and to react.

The intelligence is subtler than the mind. The function of the intelligence is to discriminate. If the mind sees a beautiful object through the senses, it thinks, "I want it." Then the intelligence starts figuring out ways to get that object.

Subtler than the intelligence is the ego. It is the ego that identifies with this whole phenomenon of intelligence, mind and the gross body and thinks that all of it is me.

Beyond the ego is the soul. The soul is the real you. The soul is the person. The soul is the observer, the witness. The soul is the source of life. When the soul identifies that "I am eternal, full of knowledge, full of bliss; I am a part of God, an instrument of God", then he is fully enlightened.

Therefore, the nature of the pure soul is to use the body, the mind, the intelligence and the ego in a spirit of compassion and love for the world, as an instrument of God's love. That is the true function of the soul in this world.

Real Freedom

In both the auspicious and the inauspicious events of life there are divine messages to be understood: the reality of material life, the reality of the kingdom of God and the lessons of how we can achieve freedom from captivity.

In every situation, we must learn to be very humble and cry out for the mercy of God. Whether we are big and wealthy in society or small and poor, we are all prisoners. Factually, the whole world is under the subjugation of illusion, which is simply controlling us. So, if we want real freedom, we have to protect ourselves by chanting God's names and by having our mind fixed on the goal of reaching Him.

The Quest for Truth

Sometimes it is said that man is a rational animal. Now, if you take away the rationality, man is an animal. Now, what does it mean to be rational? Rational means to be able to discriminate what is truth. If we do not live for the truth, if we do not live on the basis of the truth, then our whole life is a waste. It is an illusion. There will be no fruit of happiness. There wiil be no real purpose to our life. "Man is a rational animal" means man has the power to discriminate: What is the truth? What is knowledge? Who am I? And what is the purpose of life? Someone may say that this kind of life is very impractical in today's society, which is a society of competition and of "might is right." But let us examine within our hearts: what do we really want in life? There is nothing wrong with competition. But one must compete in pursuance of the truth, not on the principle of illusion and ignorance.

So, whatever our field of activity is in this world, that

is not bad. But we must act on the basis of truth. There is nothing more glorious than truth. But there is only one problem in this world, i.e. ignorance. Every other problem in this world is only due to the presence of ignorance, because the human society is in ignorance. Even in the name of faith people are attached to so many traditions, so many rituals, but as far as the real goal of life, practically everyone is ignorant. Therefore, we have to ask ourselves: what happiness, what purpose, what goal have we accomplished?

The greatest misfortune in all of creation is to get human life and to waste its precious moments by not pursuing the truth. If one is working but if one's ambition is simply sense enjoyment, such a human being is not a rational animal. Whether you are an industrialist or a doctor or a lawyer or a housewife or a professor or an administrator or a manager, if your motivation is based on the truth, if it is based on love, mercy and compassion towards all living beings, you will be most effective. Your purpose will bring about real satisfaction in your life and you can contribute real satisfaction and real happiness to the world.

Experiencing Spirituality

Theory without experience and realization has little or no value.

I was speaking once to a prestigious man having two PhDs from Cornell University, who described to me the difference between material science and spiritual science.

"In material sciences," he said, "the best that anyone can ever come up with is some intellectual proof of a theory. But there is no experience of this truth beyond intellectualization. For example, you can prove that, if you mix hydrogen with oxygen in different parts, you get water. But until you drink that water, your thirst cannot be quenched. An intellectual understanding of water is not enough; you have to drink the water to experience it."

"On the other hand, in spiritual science," he continued "you can have direct perception and experience at all times."

By experiencing and realizing the truths lying within us and God's presence within us, and sharing that with the world and finding joy in that, we can make a true and glorious contribution to the society. Let us build the foundation of our career on truth, on the spiritual science of purification of our consciousness and the awareness of our relationship with God.

Hijackers of the Soul

Human life is like a wonderful airship meant to take us to our ultimate destination. There are six hijackers in the form of lust, envy, anger, pride, greed and delusion. These enemies are living right within our hearts and it is their attempt to somehow or the other hijack the soul and bring the airplane of human life to the material conception of existence.

Then the atma becomes like a hostage. Atma means the body, the mind and the soul. All three become hostages of these hijackers and it becomes very difficult to escape.

Truth

Sincere people want to approach religion to learn how to love and how to be good to others. All great scriptures of all religions and all true saints of the world teach, not to become a Muslim, Christian, Hindu, Jew, or a Buddhist, but to gain knowledge of the "Truth."

Truth cannot be different in different places and at different times. Truth is a universal principle. What we learn in colleges today are relative truths that are very important in our practical everyday lives: how to be a good engineer or a computer professional or a manager or a businessman. But what is the underlying truth? Who am I? Where am I coming from? What is consciousness? What is the goal of human life?

To understand the nature of consciousness within us is truth. Every part of our body is changing; even our mind is changing to some extent. But there is something constant throughout these changes, and that is our consciousness.

Therefore, when we talk about religion, we are not talking about some beliefs or a blind faith or a particular set of rituals. We are talking about a science that gives us an understanding and an experience of truth—the underlying truth within us and within all. That truth harmonizes humanity and all living beings. Without that truth all harmony seems to have little or no value.

Mind Games

The mind is the best friend of man but potentially his worst enemy too. The mind that is controlled is one's best, most well-wishing friend. But the mind that is uncontrolled is one's worst enemy. In fact, there is no other enemy but our own mind. Living in this world, we have so much opposition coming our way. There may be people who are trying to even destroy us, be it individually or in business or the nation. This world is full of so many friends and enemies.

We make friends with those persons whom either we can exploit very nicely or who agree with us in our principle of how to enjoy in this world. And someone who is opposed to our conception of enjoyment in this world becomes our enemy. This is the way of the world: how to get the most sense enjoyment, how to get the most benefits from those who are our friends and how to defeat and defend against our enemies. But these are all just different mental conceptions. These are all the results of the uncontrolled mind. The mind is very difficult to control because by nature it is very envious. Because of ignorance, envy takes its seat within our mind and we suffer.

So this is the greatest need in human society, a change of mind, a purification of consciousness. Let us not be a part of the problem but let us be a part of the solution to the problem. This is real self–management: learning to control our mind. Learn to make friends with our mind by following spiritual discipline in our life and keeping holy association. And then we can enjoy the treasure of peace and real happiness, and we can distribute the contents of that treasure to our loved ones and to the world. That is the goal of life.

KNOW GOD

Is There a God?

Is everything coming from something or is everything coming from nothing?

Now, in our scientific investigation and in our practical perception of the world around us, have we ever found anything coming from nothing?

Where do you come from? From your father and mother. And where did they come from? Their father and mother. Where does the tree come from? From a seed. And where does the seed come from? Another tree.

So when everything within creation that anyone has ever seen is originating from something, then would it be logical or scientific to say that ultimately everything comes from nothing?

Nothing within our experience comes from nothing, what then to speak of the entire universe, which is operating in such an incredibly scientific manner. The technology of one's own body is greater than the best computers man has ever made. Have those computers just come from nothing?

If everything comes from something, then that "something" is the definition of God. The ancient literatures explain that God is the Absolute Truth from whom everything emanates. Obviously, that "something" from which everything emanates is not something ordinary like us. That "something" is much greater.

The different books of knowledge like Bhagavad-Gita, Koran, Bible, etc, which we know of, are the messages coming from that "something" —God.

Does God Give Freedom?

If God didn't give us freedom and He simply programmed us to love Him, then we would be computers. But God gives us the freedom to love Him, or love anybody else, or hate Him or betray Him or rebel against Him. We have the freedom to do whatever we want. We can go on and be a murderer right after reading this. We can go to a movie or to a temple. We can dance or get drunk. We have the freedom to do any of these things.

Does a computer have freedom? A computer has no freedom. A computer is simply programmed to do exactly what the computer operator wants. God does not want to live with computers. He wants to live with people. Therefore, He has given us freedom and independence.

Our freedom is whether we want to accept or reject the grace of God.

Dependent and Independent Truth

Dependent or Relative truth means that truth which is interdependent on a previous truth to exist. Why do we call our family members relatives? Because we are relative to one another. My father is relative to me. My existence is relative to his existence, and his existence is relative to his father's existence. We are all relatives to one another; that means we are interdependent on one another for each other's existence. That is the dependent or relative truth.

Now, the source of all relative truths cannot be a relative truth; it has to be the absolute truth or independent truth. Ultimately, either everything comes from nothing or everything comes from the absolute truth; everything cannot come from another relative truth. And if we accept that everything comes from the absolute truth or independent truth—which is more logical and scientifically consistent with our perception that everything does not come from nothing—then we have to study that absolute truth. Bhagavad-Gita is the scientific study of that absolute truth.

When we come to the level of the absolute truth, then there is no beginning and no end. This is because it is the source of all relativity, and it is transcendental—beyond relativity.

God's Special Effects

We wake up in the night and we find ourselves in the middle of the most incredible feature film right before our eyes. There is an unending 360-degree movie theater all around us. God is revealing incredible miracles at every stage.

Show me any special effect that can be compared to the sky at night, studded with the luminous moon and innumerable stars. We are able to see them although they are billions of miles away. Can anyone except God do something like this?

Miracles of God

No man can ever imitate what God has done. What can we create? What can we maintain? And what can we destroy?

How are the planets floating in perfect order? How is the sun lighting up the sky in all directions in the entire universe? How are all creatures on earth growing and creating? When we eat, how is our food getting digested?

Everywhere we turn, God is revealing miracles to us. Life is full of God's miracles, but we are so blind that we can't see them. If someone comes before us and produces gold, we think, "My God! How wonderful! This is a miracle." But the shining of the sun, the rains from the clouds, the planets in the sky moving in perfect orbits are massive miracles. Just the fact that you have a child that is growing is a miracle. How he gets his energy when he eats is a miracle. No man can ever create this.

When we get the vision to see God's greatness, it

attracts our consciousness back to our loving relationship with Him.

Pure Love from a Perfect God

Whatever God does is perfect and complete.

What is most perfect? Pure, unmotivated and uninterrupted love. Nothing can be more perfect than that.

The Absolute Truth's being perfect and complete means that whatever is emanating from Him is based on the principle of the purest, highest, most unmotivated and uninterrupted love. Even the wrath of God is based on pure unalloyed love, because whatever God does is for the welfare of all living beings. Just like the sun showers its beneficial rays upon everyone without discrimination, God's love is available to one and all without discrimination.

Whether one is a terrible dacoit or a great saintly person, God's love is equal to everyone. There is only one difference. The Lord reciprocates with the saintly person in all sweetness, because the saintly person approaches the Lord with love. The Lord expresses His love for the dacoit by smashing him for having gone against His laws. Ultimately, God wants all living entities to come back to Him. The path of Bhakti, loving devotional service, is the direct express highway back home, back to the kingdom of God.

A Loving God

When we see people suffering terribly, it is very bewildering. Why is God doing this to people? Superficially, it seems very cruel and unfair. However, the reality is altogether different.

Every action must have an equal and opposite reaction. That is the law of karma. Sufferings and miseries are the manifestation of our indulgence in sinful activities from the past. We may or may not remember those activities.

This stringent law of karma, designed and orchestrated by God, is His unmotivated, uninterrupted love for the soul going through it. Physically it may be cruel, but for the soul, it is like the love of a parent for the child's own benefit. A child who is told that his parents are punishing him because they love him, cannot accept or understand it. But an adult can very well understand. When we grow spiritually, we see that there is nothing but God's love, pervading everything and everywhere.

The perfection of life is not to be free from physical or mental suffering, because the body and the mind are going to suffer today or tomorrow no matter what we do. The perfection of life is the ability to perceive and appreciate God's love in every single aspect of this creation. The perfection of life is to be grateful for God's love—no matter what way, shape or form it comes—knowing that, according to what we have done, this is God's way of bringing us closer to Him. This is not some blind faith. Nor is it just a superimposition of some nice philosophy to cope with the problems of life. This is the Supreme Truth—truth that has been revealed by all the great incarnations, scriptures and saints.

Deity and Omnipresent God

Many times people ask, "If God is omnipresent, why worship a Deity?"

If God is omnipresent, is He not present in the Deity

as well? If we are honest and realistic, we can very easily understand that to fix our mind on God who is present everywhere and in everything is indeed difficult. Therefore, the Lord out of His mercy and kindness reveals Himself to us through wonderful mediums by which we can completely absorb our consciousness in Him.

One such medium is His name. The name is the Deity of God in sound that we can carry with us everywhere.

The Deity in the temple is another manifestation that God has so kindly given us to completely focus our mind and senses in serving Him. In His Deity form we can bathe God, we can feed God, we can meditate on His beauty, we can completely absorb our attention in Him.

Deity worship is a most wonderful sublime form of meditation that awakens our natural serving potency and our love for God. God has given the Deity as a wonderful facility and opportunity for us to fix our mind on Him and to love Him and serve Him.

Temple of the Heart

Chanting the name of God is the most sublime process. If it is possible, set up a little temple in your home. If it is not, still the name of God can be worshiped in the temple of your heart.

Gifts of God

Our work is pure when we realize that we are not the doers but are simply instruments in the hands of God to do His will. As long as we think "I am the doer of good work", we become proud and contaminated.

God is the doer. If God did not give me the air, could I breathe? If God did not give the sun, could I see? If God did not give the rains, could I drink water or eat food? If God did not give the earth, could I survive?

Everything that we are made of is a gift of God. Neither our forefathers nor the scientists have created the things that we are surviving on: the sunlight, the air, the rain, the earth, the food grains and our very body. Our mother and father did not produce this body. They were just instruments. It is not that our father invented the seed of life by his own intelligence. God invented the seed of life and put it within the father who is just the instrument of God to put that seed in the mother.

God made the womb. The mother did not make her womb. The mother's womb is an instrument of God to let that seed, which He planted, grow. God has given us birth. God has made every hair on our head and every pore on our body. He has created it all and given us everything we require to sustain our lives.

Moon-Like God

When the big, dark cloud of ignorance enters in our lives and covers the full moon of God's presence in our hearts, it leaves not just our own life but also the whole world in darkness.

What is within reflects in everything without. A person's consciousness within is manifested everywhere through his or her eyes, ears, and all of the senses. If we see the beauty of God within our own lives, we see the beauty of God everywhere through our senses. But, if there is darkness in our hearts, if we are forgetful of God, then we will see only darkness everywhere. This is a beautiful lesson to be learnt. When our hearts are free of the clouds of ignorance, everything appears to us like a clearly visible autumn night.

Let the moon-like God come into our hearts to dispel all darkness and fear. Let our hearts be like the clear skies, free from the clouds of ignorance. When we perceive all living beings to be like the brilliant shining stars and God to be like the full moon, then there is actual beauty and love in our lives.

WISDOM FROM THE HEART

Two Things to Forget! Two to Remember!

Two things to forget forever are:

a) Anything bad anyone has done unto us: To the extent that we are willing to forgive and forget, God will forgive us. Forgiveness is a great virtue.

b) Anything good that we have done unto others: If we remember our good deeds, we become proud, and that pride ruins everything. We should think that we are only delivery persons, delivering the goods. God wants us to simply be a delivery person. Ultimately, God does it all.

Two things to always remember are:

a) Death: Death can come at any moment, whether one is an insignificant ant crawling on the floor or the future Head of State of the biggest democracy of the world.

b) God's Holy Name: Since death can come at any moment, the other thing that we should remember is the Lord's Holy Name, because His mercy is fully revealed through His Name eternally.

hope in pain

Whatever God does is ultimately a miracle for our pleasure. Even the punishments are ultimately for our pleasure even though they may cause pains in our bodies. Biologically, what is pain? Different nerve endings go through certain transformations that create signals, which come out as pain. It is an unbelievable creation.

Even pain is God's miracle. Technologically it is so complex that even the greatest machine cannot create such a thing as pain.

Pain is specifically designed and minutely created by God for our pleasure. Ultimately, everything is for the pleasure of the soul, to bring us, souls, back to God's original abode. Everything that takes place in our life is God revealing His miraculous, incredible mercy upon us. The entire existence is simply a reciprocation of love between God and His children.

true culture

Culture is the humility, the morality and the wisdom of the heart, expressed through lifestyles and arts. Culture is not just how you dress or what music you listen to. One of Hitler's number two men was one of the mastermind demons responsible for ordering and murdering tens and millions of innocent people. That was his work.

Nevertheless, in his private life he was considered to be such a cultured gentleman. He wore the finest clothes, he had all the mannerisms of politeness, the etiquette of speaking in nice respectful ways to others, and he knew how to eat according to the very aristocratic manners. He was a patron of the fine arts, he loved classical music and he gave so much in charity to promote classical music and poetry and theatre. From every way of looking at what we consider culture, he was a very cultured gentleman. He spoke sweetly and he did all the things that the high echelon's cultural society respects and adores.

However in his heart, he was such a ruthless murderer that he tortured and slaughtered millions of innocent children, women, and helpless men even if they were old. So true culture is not just about your lifestyle or art, but is essentially about your lifestyle and art actually embodying the principles of humility, morality and wisdom of the heart.

With Every Rising and Setting of the Sun

The most valuable thing we have in life is every precious moment that God has given us. Time is priceless. Money, estate, or even reputation, if lost, can be gained back by hard work. But one moment that is wasted, cannot be brought back for all the wealth in the entire creation.

Time and tide wait for no man. As little kids in school, it seemed like centuries even when we were just waiting for the weekend. But, as we grow old, days pass like minutes. Soon we are at the threshold of departing from this particular body. We look back and think, "Where has my life gone? It seems like it has only been a moment!"

Therefore, we must understand the value of every precious moment. How we invest each moment of our life is the most important consideration of our human intelligence. We should utilize every moment to the greatest benefit of ourselves as well as of others. The scriptures explain that with every rising and setting of the sun we are one day closer to death. But for those who utilize their precious time to understand the true purpose of life and to hear and chant the glories of the Supreme Lord, every rising and setting of the sun brings them one day closer to eternal life.

The Power of Inquiry

One great saintly personality remarked that everyone spends their lives within a series of questions and answers. When a bird rises in the morning, it begins asking questions and searching for answers. When it comes back to the nest at night, it is still asking questions and trying to find answers. In human society the businessmen, politicians, lawyers, artists, farmers etc., all are seeking answers to their questions.

Life is a series of questions and answers:

How to solve our problems?

How to find happiness?

How to avoid suffering?

How to make friends?

How to gain power and prestige?

Of course, in today's age the series of questions and answers is mostly about how to make money.

All the television shows, cinemas, newspapers, magazines, are about these questions and answers.

The Vedic scriptures explain that, now that you are a human being, inquire about who you are. The questions about eating, sleeping, mating and defending and all of their various sub-divisions exhibit the basic trend of human intelligence in today's world, but these are unimportant questions.

Who am I?

Why am I suffering?

Where am I coming from?

Where am I going?

Who is God?

What is the nature of this universe?

What is my relationship with God within this universe?

When a human being comes to the elevated platform of making serious inquiry on these subjects, then human life has real spiritual value.

If we really want to digest food, we have to have hunger. If we have no hunger, we have very weak digestion. Hunger is a very important part of life because it gives power to digest and that principle holds true for spiritual knowledge as well. When we feel the urgency and the hunger to solve the real problems of life and we inquire from people who act truly and who reveal the word of God in an unadulterated way, then our human life really begins.

The scriptures tell us that there is a final exam. That final exam is called death. It's not a horrible thing unless we fail it. Death is neither good nor bad. If we fail the exam of death it's a miserable situation. But if we pass that exam it's the most glorious opportunity in all of creation. We can pass this examination by using our life to seek answers to the questions of the purpose of life and then following those answers which will lead us to the right path and destination of our life.

Real Medicine

In material life, there are natural insurmountable catastrophes. A few years ago in India, in Gujarat there was a massive earthquake. Tens and thousands of people died in just a matter of minutes. The earthquake lasted for only 45 seconds. Millions of dollars worth damage occurred and thousands of lives were lost. From our Bhaktivedanta hospital in Mumbai, when medical staff reached the earthquake site, there were queues of people coming with crushed heads and broken limbs; it was horrible. Doctors were treating them, and the whole while there was soothing divine music and sanctified food distribution also going on. Every evening, there were discourses in the local Gujarati language on Bhagavad-Gita. For the morning and evening classes, they had erected a pandal, a temporary make-shift cloth structure. Many people reiterated that the classes and the divine music were giving more relief than all the medical work.

It was a tragedy on every level: physical, mental, emotional and spiritual. When your mother is dead, your father is dead, your brothers and sisters are dead, your children are dead, your husband is dead, your wife is dead, and you have seen them all die right before your eyes, you have seen every bit of your property that you gave your whole life to, devastated, then you have nothing more left. Just from the 45 seconds of the earth shaking. If you went to the relief camps, you could see how people were really suffering; they were dazed and confused. They didn't know what to do, where to go, where they were coming from. Their life, and everything they had worked for—family, loved ones, property—was gone; there was nothing left. So the doctors tried to fix their broken arms, but what about their minds, what about their hearts, what about their lives? The doctors fixed their broken legs, the relief workers helped them bury their loved ones. What they were really doing is bandaging people, doing some orthopedic surgery on different people's limbs and physically they were setting them alright, but they were unable to fix their devastated lives. They had nothing to live for any more. However, when these same people, after getting their arms, legs, ribs fixed up, came to the pandal and heard the soothing divine music and the teachings of Bhagavad-Gita, they found hope, they found a meaning to life, they found a way to deal with their broken hearts and actually attain an eternal destination. So many people came and said this is the actual relief work, that we were healing their hearts, we were healing their souls. There were thousands of organizations that were fixing their bodies, which was a laudable and noble work. But when they came to us the villagers said that we were trying to heal their hearts and souls and we had given them hope and the ultimate highest reason to live and we had taught them how to deal with this situation and to transcend it. They were so grateful. They didn't want us to leave. So, this is what people really need.

Whether they are physically injured or whether they are physically fit, their hearts are crippled if they don't know who they are and what is their relationship with God. We try to make use of material nature in the best way we can, but ultimately our real purpose is to help people transcend the material nature. If somehow or the other, before imminent death comes, if people learn how to love and serve to whatever extent they can, that is the greatest gift.

FROM NATURE

The Ocean

During summer, very little water comes from the river into the ocean, but that does not dry up the ocean. During monsoon, sometimes the river becomes several miles wide and billions of liters of water pour in every minute in the ocean, but that does not flood the ocean.

In either case, the ocean remains unaffected. That is because the ocean is so full and deep in itself that no external forces can disturb its stillness and equilibrium.

Compare the ocean with a puddle of water. During the summer, it becomes completely dried up, and during the monsoons, it floods over. Why? Because it lacks the depth of the ocean.

If you are full and deep within, none of the external forces can disturb you. But if you are empty, you are completely affected by everything that comes in your life.

"A person who is not disturbed by the incessant flow of desires—that enter like rivers into the ocean, which is ever being filled but is always still—can alone achieve peace, and not the man who strives to satisfy such desires."

—Bhagavad-Gita As It Is 2.70

Rains

The rainwater that pours from the sky is crystal clear. But when it comes in contact with the ground, it becomes muddy. The question is: what is the nature of water? Is it clear or muddy? It is clear, but when it gets mixed with other things, it appears muddy.

We simply have to separate what is not water, the contaminating agents, from water. That is the process of filtration. When we filter water, all the dirt gets trapped in the filter and the water revives its clear and pure state once again.

Similarly, our consciousness is by nature eternal, full of knowledge and full of bliss, joy and pleasure. However, like rainwater, our consciousness is now mixed with many superficial external impurities. Through the process of filtration, by the chanting of

God's names, our consciousness becomes clear and transparent. With clear consciousness, we can perceive God, we can experience happiness, and we find peace within. In fact, there is no other way by which we can find peace.

calm caves

It is interesting how in both Eastern and Western spirituality great renounced persons would often perform their prayer and worship in the caves of the mountains. It is in the spirit of simplicity and renunciation— simplicity in that it's completely natural, it is provided by God Himself. There is no need to pay any rent or to work for accommodation. In fact, the ancient scriptures say, "What is the use of so much effort to build houses when there are so many caves in the mountains? What is the use of pillows when you have two arms to put your head on? Why struggle for all kinds of clothes when there's bark of trees you could wear?"

If we look for happiness in accumulating material wealth or property, then it's an endless cycle of aspiration and frustration. The more we make our life simple, the more it becomes natural to be God conscious. The idea is, when life becomes very extraneous with efforts for obtaining mundane things, it distracts our attention away from our spiritual pursuits.

So, when great saints and sages would come to these caves, it would be to disassociate themselves from the modes of passion and ignorance, to detach themselves from the passionate world of greed and lust, and in that situation to be able to completely put their full attention into prayer and the chanting of the Holy Names and the study of scriptures.

Mother Earth

Everything we have is coming from the earth. Our bodies, foods, homes, books and even our computers are all ultimately coming from the earth.

When we see a beautiful lotus flower, what do we immediately feel? The first thought that should come to the mind is, "What a beautiful miracle!"

A little brown seed is sown in brown soil, and then

watered by the rains.And what comes out is a beautiful pink lotus, very smooth and soft in texture and very aromatic in fragrance. No man can make anything like this, no matter how hard he tries. We can try to imitate, but we cannot make fragrance like this. And it's just coming out of the ground. Even great scientists cannot do this. So, this is one of the innumerable miracles that mother nature unfolds every day. We just need to be conscious of them. If we are eagerly seeking, mother nature will reveal amazing miracles.

Water for Life

The earth's wealth is in the form of water, because nothing can survive without water. Without water, there is no food. We may have big refineries and factories, but we cannot drink oil, nor can we eat motorcars. We need food. The food grains are born of rain. No rain, no food. No rain, no fortune.

The Holy Name is like water. Hearing and chanting the glories of the Lord is the water that nourishes the dried-up heart and allows the seed of love of God to grow. The Holy Name is the mercy of God; it is like the rain. When we taste the Holy Name with our tongue, the tongue, which is like a dried-up desert, becomes full of life. When that name enters into our ears, it gives so much refreshment, nourishment and relief that we desire millions and millions of ears. When the sweet sound of the nectarean name enters into our heart, it gives complete bliss and satisfaction, and our senses become inert by tasting its sweetness.

The Cooling Moon

The moon is considered the very symbol of beauty in this world.

When the Lord appears in His various manifestations, His beauty is unparalleled, inconceivable and unlimited. The only possible phenomenon in this world that He can be compared to is the full moon. What is so special about the full moon is that it gives light that is very cooling, refreshing and nourishing. Just as the moon gives light and coolness in the darkness of night, similarly the remembrance of the Lord gives light, refreshes our hearts, our minds and our very souls, even in the darkness of this world.

Seeing Through the Ears

With every blooming of a flower, with every song of a bird, in both the sorrows and the joys of life, we can find great fulfillment if we understand what God is trying to teach us.

My spiritual teacher, Srila Prabhupada, taught a very simple principle, which brings great fulfillment and excitement to life. He told us, "We should always see through the eyes of ancient wisdom. A learned person does not see with his eyes; he sees with his ears."

We must learn to process the information that we witness in the world around us through the knowledge that we have acquired from the ancient literatures and the great saints of the past.

Anything that happens in this world—in our own lives, in the lives of those who are around us, in the national or in the world—we should try to interpret it in such a way that it gives us real understanding and realization. This is how we should always be absorbed in this world, trying to hear the word of God in everything around us.

Clouds and Moon

During the rainy season, we cannot see the moon because it is covered by the clouds. The clouds, however, are radiant with the glow of the moon's rays. Similarly, in our material existence we cannot directly perceive the soul, because our consciousness is covered by the cloud-like false ego, the false identification with the material world and the material body.

The Bhagavad-Gita describes that the energy of the soul is consciousness. When this consciousness is manifested through the screen of the false ego, it appears as dull material consciousness in which there is no direct vision of the soul or God.

We think that material consciousness is full of hope and happiness. This is comparable to thinking that the luminous clouds are lighting up the night sky. Actually, the clouds are dark and they hamper the moonshine; they appear luminous only because they are filtering the brilliant rays of the moon.

Similarly, at times material consciousness appears pleasurable or enlightened because it is filtering the original bliss and enlightened consciousness coming directly from the soul. The false ego hampers and obstructs the real spiritual consciousness, which is fully enlightened and peaceful.

Swan-like persons

A swan can separate milk from a mixture of milk and water. Also, its mind is fixed on attaining the nectar in the whorl of the lotus flower. Pure-hearted human beings devoted to serving God are compared to swans because they have the ability to extract the essence from everything they come in contact with, and also because their minds are fixed on attaining the nectar of true love of God.

The honeybee and the fly

The honeybee flies from one flower to the next, drinking only the sweetness and the essence of the nectar of that flower without disturbing the flower in the slightest, and then going to the next flower and drinking the nectar there. So, we have much to learn from the honeybee; it is teaching us the art of transcending the faults in others. A honeybee looks for flowers even in a place full of garbage. Not paying attention to all the filth around, the honeybee rushes to even a small flower amidst the garbage and sucks the nectar from it. The qualification of a true spiritualist is that he or she has given up the propensity to find faults in others.

However bad, evil or crooked a man or woman may be in this world, a saintly person can always find something good in them. He magnifies that good quality hundreds and thousands of times, and simply flies over anything that does not provide him nectar, just like the honeybee.

We are living in an age when people are very quick to criticize, to find faults, to gossip, to relish rumors of others' defects. But a saintly person knows, as Lord Jesus Christ has described in the Bible, "Seek and ye shall find", that if you look for the nectar, you will find the nectar. If you look for the faults, the flaws, the disgusting matter, then that is all you will see. For example, the moon is shining beautifully every night emanating volumes and volumes of cooling, soothing rays. Only a fool will look at the moon and condemn it for having so many spots. The honeybee is not concerned with the spots. The honeybee is only looking for the nectar. So a saintly person should always look for the good in others. Even if there is just a tiny little spark of good in another, the saintly person wants to fan that spark and make it grow and grow until it blazes and devours all the bad qualities.

We can learn something from the fly too. In this world we can learn our lessons from both the good and the bad. The fly is not interested in the flower.

If your body is very healthy and you have one cut that is infected, the fly will zoom right in to eat your infectious pus. It doesn't care about your healthy parts. It's simply looking for the pus. This is the life of the fly. How many flies do you see drinking the nectar from flowers, and how many bees do we find eating the pus? So, one whose mentality is like that of a fly is always looking for the pus in others, always quick to find faults, to criticize, to condemn, to discuss obnoxious rumors.

Be Like a Tree

Tolerating the heat of the sun, the cold snow of the winter, the wind and rain in the monsoons, the tree is simply supplying all benefits to others:

supplying shade to us, while it suffers in the sun; supplying firewood to warm us, while it suffers in the freezing winter. Although it stands alone without a home, it provides its limbs in the form of wood for us to build houses to live in.

Trees are immersed in the mood of service to all living entities without discrimination. They are compassionate.

This is the standard of a saintly person: to be like a tree, always willing to accept all kinds of inconveniences to bring happiness and relief to others. A saintly person is not so concerned with his or her own problems, but is more concerned with others' problems. If we do not care about others' problems, then we drown in our own problems, which are endless and which bring down our consciousness. But if we are concerned with others' problems, then we don't have time to think about our own problems. This is a saint: like a tree, always eager to serve others, in all regards, in every possible way.

Caterpillar

There is a story of a boy who had a good heart. Once this boy saw a caterpillar in his garden. He began to carefully observe it. He found that the caterpillar was in a difficult situation. It was bound by a cocoon and was struggling to release itself from this cocoon. It strove very hard to come out of it. But try as it may, it was not able to come out of it even by a centimeter. But it never gave up its efforts. It tried and tried.

This boy was moved by the effort of the caterpillar and, having a heart filled with compassion, decided to help the caterpillar in its suffering. He ran inside his house and got a pair of scissors and slowly and carefully cut the cocoon of the caterpillar and released it.

What did he see when he cut the cocoon? He saw that the caterpillar was actually developing wings to become a butterfly. And because he had cut the cocoon before time, the wings of the caterpillar were very weak. They did not have the strength to handle the weight of the caterpillar and so the caterpillar could not fly.

Similarly, sometimes when we struggle in our lives, it may seem painful to someone who is watching. But those very struggles actually make us strong and powerful. Many people ask, "Why does God allow us to suffer?" We can learn from this boy; if he had allowed the caterpillar to suffer a little more, then it would have soared to the sky, flown from one flower to another and been appreciated by the world for its colors and beauty.

As You Sow, So Shall You Reap

Life is so shallow, so superficial and actually very lonely when you have so much, but you don't really know who loves you and who doesn't, and who is using you. On the other hand, persons who are loved for their integrity and their compassion, are actually respected. There is substance and realness to that. In order to have actual integrity, we have to build our life on a foundation, that is scientific, logical and philosophical, that is based on truth, that we can turn to for protecting us from selling our souls to the deranged nature of ourselves and others. If we can cleanse our hearts, we realize the great glorious foundation that is within us and upon finding it, we can build our life upon it. Then, we will find the ultimate truth in everything we do and say, and we can lead the world in that light.

Now, it appears, why would one want to be righteous? It is much better to be bad. Some people ask, "Why do good things happen to bad people and bad things to good people?" Actually, as you sow, so shall you reap. As you do, so shall you get the result. It is just a matter of time. Consider the example of a silo, a grain storage container, in which we put the grains from the top and take them out from the bottom. So, people put very good grains in, that is, they do righteous activities, virtuous activities. But then often due to bad association, they lower themselves to their dark side and then they commit deviant acts, greedy acts; they become cheaters, rogues and then it's the dirty rotten grains that they are putting in. So for now, they may be getting the good grains that they had put in earlier. But in due course of time, all the rotten grains are going to come out. There is another person who might have done impious activities in the past, but having learnt his lesson, became very righteous and very good. He may be getting rotten things now, but the future is very bright, auspicious and glorious for him.

So we can't judge things just by how they appear to our eyes. We must understand philosophically how the world works, then we will get the understanding of what the future holds based on what a person does and how that person lives.

Entangling Web

The network of material illusion has been created with great sophistication. Every time we deviate from the principle of servitude, we become more and more entangled in the complexities of material bondage. It is a vicious cycle. Every thought, word and deed, performed in an attempt to find happiness apart from our service to God, further binds us, covers us and entangles us in ignorance.

It's like a fly that is caught in a spider's web. Somehow or the other it is entangled, but out of ignorance it thinks that it can get itself out of that situation. The more it moves around to free itself, the more it becomes entangled in the web. The enthusiastic fly moves around, struggling hard to free itself. But after some time we don't even see the fly;

all we see is a little web-ball that's just moving around. The fly is now totally bound and covered.

Human life is meant for self-realization, not for entangling ourselves like that fly in the spider's web. The only way a fly can get out is if somebody comes and takes it off. And for those entangled in ignorance, that help comes from the saintly people.

The Most Dangerous Creature

Among the innumerable creatures of the world, two are most deadly: the serpent and the envious human being. Of the two who do you think is more dangerous?

A great spiritual teacher said, "The reason why a serpent is less dangerous is because you can tame a serpent using different herbs and mantras."

But nothing can make an envious person nice. A serpent bites only if it is threatened and the most it can do is kill only one person at a time. The reaction of the serpent is not out of envy but out of self-protection. It wants to either protect itself or its offspring.

Human beings, on the other hand, are building bombs by which they can kill millions of people at a time for no reason except to protect their false egos. So who is more dangerous?

IRONY OF THIS WORLD

Power of Credit Cards

Credit cards, which are in one sense just little pieces of plastic, have the value of thousands of dollars. All you have to do to buy things is just show this card.

On one hand, credit cards make life easy in buying things. But on the other hand, they are also one of the greatest sources of miseries in society. Because when you have these cards, you get infatuated with the sense of power and wealth.

You start thinking, “Now I can buy anything. I can do anything. I can travel anywhere.” And the problem is, you do it. But, then a month later, the bill comes. You can't pay the bill with a piece of plastic. Then you have to go out to struggle and work. Sometimes I have seen people doing two or three jobs just to pay the debts they have incurred from using their credit cards indiscriminately. I know of a person who incurred such a debt ten years ago. For the past ten years, this poor soul has been working as a slave to pay back the debt, and to this day he is not even close to it.

This little plastic card hardly weighs a few grams. But when you start using it, the result is a massive mountainous burden of debt and anxiety that crushes your life.

Power brings responsibility. The greater the power in hand, the greater is the responsibility. Understand the power of this small plastic card and act responsibly instead of getting carried away by this manmade illusion.

Manmade Illusion

Many times people visit amusement parks, stand in lines and pay so much money just to see a robotically-animated historical personality deliver a speech.

Why do people stand in a line? All around them are so many people blinking their eyes, moving their hands and speaking. What's going on inside in the animatronics theater with a robot of a historical figure speaking or moving is also going on outside all around them. But people are just so bored to death outside with other people around them that they go to visit an animatronics show to see the same things.

The statue inside may be programmed to move and even speak, but it cannot think and feel. Thousands of people all over are doing everything that the statue does—and doing it millions of times better, and with thoughts and feelings. God has created all these real people, but we won't pay a single dollar for having seen them. We will stand in a line for seven hours and pay so much money just to see a manmade statue that blinks its eyes. It is just an illusion.

God is creating so many miracles before our eyes for our pleasure and our learning. But we ignore them.

Listen to Good Advice

My father told me that when he was young, nobody had the slightest idea that cigarettes were bad. It was fashionable to smoke cigarettes. One movie star always had a cigarette hanging out of his mouth. Everyone in America was trying to imitate the way he did it. He was such a handsome man and his style became the fashion. Eventually however, he died of cancer of the lips. One of the most famous singers would sing while smoking a cigarette. It was amazing how someone could sing while smoking, but he died of lung cancer when he was only forty.

So doctors began coming up with slogans saying, "Cigarettes kill you. Stop Smoking!"

When these messages came out, cigarette smoking became even more popular amongst the youth. Why? Because they were trying to prove to themselves, "I am daring. I am fearless. I don't care if I am risking my life. I am going to do it to be cool. Yes, I know it will kill me. So what?"

Let us begin to see the world around us and learn from the past mistakes. Let us begin listening to good advice, rather than challenging it and destroying ourselves.

Rain of Mercy

Material existence is like a burning forest fire. It is burning our hearts. Who can say that their hearts are not burning due to the anxieties of material life? All our attempts for relief and happiness in this world are consumed by this burning, blazing forest fire. All of our successes and credible accomplishments are ultimately evaporated by the sun of material existence.

In this difficult situation, people are suffering. Spiritually-minded people pray for God to come into their lives and relieve them of the pains and sufferings of this existence.

After a long stretch of being burnt by the sun and the forest fire of material existence, the onset of the beautiful blackish rain clouds brings great hope. We feel refuge; we feel sheltered. The blackness in the rain clouds indicates the presence of rain, the rain of God's mercy. That rain is the nourishing, life-giving mercy that relieves us from the heat of the sun and gives nourishment to all living beings. When God comes, the rains of His mercy fill our lives. Then all wonderful fortune and happiness from within are bestowed upon us by His divine mercy.

The hole in the heart

In the gulf of Mexico there is oil coming out of the ground. This is the biggest news in America. Tens of thousands of gallons of oil are coming out into the ocean everyday. People are trying to stop it, but are failing. It is considered to be one of the worst manmade disasters in the history of America. And it may take hundreds of years for that area to recover ecologically. And the oil company says that the hole is difficult to fix because it's very deep, about one mile into the bottom of the ocean.

However, the problem is much deeper than one mile. The problem is that deep in the people's hearts, there is a hole in their values: the hole of ahankara or ego. And from that hole the toxic oil of greed and lust and anger and pride is pouring out and polluting our consciousness. And because our consciousness is polluted, we are polluting the world. It is due to ego and greed. And even if they patch up the hole in the ocean, if they don't patch up the hole in the heart, they are just going to make another hole and another hole and another hole, and bigger problems will come.

Bhakti or devotion to God is the process of healing that hole in the heart and cleaning the toxic waste out of the heart and filling our heart with the nectar of love of God. And when that nectar fills our hearts, we can fill the whole ocean of the material world with that nectar. This is the greatest need in the human society: to clean the heart of toxic lust and greed and envy and pride and anger, and to access divine love, and to be instruments of that love. That is the greatest thing anyone can do in the world.

What do you mean by fate?

Man is the maker of his own destiny or fate. For every action there is an equal reaction. We have the choice of what action we perform, but after we perform it, we have no choice of the reaction. The reaction is our fate and we are the ones who created it.

For instance, if I go to the top of a building and jump, what is my fate while I am in the air? To hit the ground and die. That's my fate. I can't change my fate once I am in the air. But if I didn't jump at all, I would not have that fate. If I take poison, what is my fate? To die. I can't escape from my fate. But if I didn't take the poison, I would not have that fate.

If I go to the airport and get on a flight to London and one hour after the flight takes off, I say, "I do not want to go to London." What will the flight authorities say to me? "It's your fate to go to London, because you are on the plane." There is no way that you can't go to London.

Once we perform an act, we get a reaction. That is our fate. But we have the choice to decide what acts to do. If we do good things, our fate will be good. If we do bad things, our fate will be bad. Destiny is unavoidable after we make our move, after we make our decision. But we have the full spectrum of choices to educate ourselves and understand what is the best decision to make in life. Then our fate will be most auspicious and glorious.

Our past actions in this life and in previous lives influence our fate. Amongst two people who suffer the same disease and get the same medicine, one lives and the other dies. The law of karma, the law of action and reaction, takes into consideration every detail of what we are doing and what we have done, and that determines our destiny.

The Power of Time

Take a glass filled with a fizzy drink, maybe Sprite. What do you see on the surface? Lot of small bubbles that fizzle out in a few seconds. Govinda Dasa, a Bengali poet, has said that our life in this world is as temporary and insignificant as a bubble of water on a lotus petal. Hence, the scriptures implore us not to aspire for a permanent settlement in this temporary world. All advances in technology and all attempts to prolong life in this world are akin to the attempt to prolong the life of a bubble in a glass of Sprite. In comparison to the sky of eternity, our life is as brief as a flash of lightning.

An old man and a young boy may both look at the same clock, but they see it differently. An old man is apprehensive and nervous as he sees the clock ticking away. A young boy, however, is impatient and wonders when the watch will speed up so that he can enjoy life. But the old man wishes that the clock stop moving. Well, a timepiece may stop, but time won't. When bored, we want to kill time, but no one can do so. It's Mr. Time who kills all without discrimination.

I am always amazed to see the cemetery in New York. It's a huge place extending over miles. You could drive for a long time seeing all the tombstones. It seems pretty impressive, but on closer examination we see it's a sad reflection of the real world—devoid of all its glamour and glitz. A dead person is buried in an attractive casket that costs around $5000. Then there is the tombstone, which is made of granite or marble. I have a friend who's in the tombstone business and he's a millionaire. You will never go bust in this business because the market demand is always high and people are always dying. Then the dates of birth and death are written on the tombstone along with a message. A few friends drop by for a few years to remember the dead person. Although the body is buried seven feet below the ground, still the insects feast on the casket and the body. There's nothing in the cemetery about us except for the name and the years of our life. We thus become an insignificant statistic after a few years, lost in the teeming crowd of millions who are wandering in this material world.

World of Temporary Happiness

Many years back there was a newspaper article about one of the wealthiest men in the world. He had a college-going son, who was studying anthropology. He went on a project to a place in New Guinea to study man-eating cannibals. He wanted to write a book on these people and get his PhD.

After doing interviews and taking photos for his

research, he was returning back to his ship on a little boat. As he was on his way to the ship, the little boat began to sink. Finding no other way to survive, he swam across to the island. Nobody was able to trace him after that.

This rich man sent his assistants and police all over the island to look for his son, and they found that the object of the son's studies, the man-eating cannibals, ate him away. This man was devastated. On being interviewed by several newspapers he said, "With all my hundreds of millions of dollars, with all my power and influence over governments, societies and banks, with all my fame and my good health, I will never be able to find a moment of happiness in my entire life, because my son has been killed."

All the happiness of this world is temporary.

On Leadership

Ideal Taxes

By God's divine arrangement the sun extracts water from the ocean, stores it in clouds and showers it in the form of rain for the welfare of all on earth. Similarly, the duty of the government is to extracts taxes from the citizens and to distribute them for everyone's welfare.

When the leaders are not God conscious, we find that the money extracted as taxes is not returned for the welfare of the citizens. To get our own money in the form of welfare, we have to pay bribes. We never hear about the sun taking bribes to give back the water he takes from the ocean.

What does this mean? This means that the leaders, instead of ruling on behalf of God, are ruling on behalf of their own pride, ego and exploitative tendencies. Leaders who really want to do good for the people are extremely rare. Such rare leaders may have all good motives to really help. But they cannot do so, because they are not directed by holy books and saintly persons who can actually teach them the method of being in harmony with the arrangement of God.

Real Leadership

There are many books that teach you various leadership techniques to fatten your bank balance, to climb up the corporate ladder, to have more power, to control people's lives and to inflate your ego accordingly. But what about a type of leadership by which we can make a very serious, significant contribution to people's lives and to the world in general? Actual leadership means to be a leader who actually has a positive effect in people's lives—and not simply leading in such a way that you make a lot of money. What really matters is the mark that one leaves in the world. If one does not have proper integrity, the world hates him. People despise hypocrisy.

When you become a leader, people open their hearts to trust you; they open their faith. In that state you can do the greatest benefit to those people's lives, but you could also cause the greatest pain, anguish and devastation in those people's lives. So leadership is not a post to enjoy. If that is your idea, then you will be a very exploitative person and a very miserable leader. Leadership is a very serious, significant responsibility of service to others. A real leader is in a spirit of service. And, in order to be a proper leader in that way, one must have knowledge of what is actually right and what is actually wrong.

Knowledge is power. The great thing is not about having power; the great thing is how you use your power. Are you using the power in such a way that you gain genuine inner fulfillment and enlightenment, and improve the physical, emotional and ethical quality of others? If you are just going through your life thinking about job, money and prestige, then will there be any depth to your life? Will there ever be fulfillment in your life? Are you just selling your consciousness out to the world of materialism, greed, envy and pride? Is your life superficial, or is it meaningful and real? These are the most important questions that you should be asking. A good leader is a person who attracts people's confidence and enthuses people with loyalty and faithfulness because of their relationship, whether the relationship is immediate or extended.

Foundation of Leadership

There are many books and courses on modern leadership qualities, where they speak about various virtues one should cultivate: patience rather than impatience, genuinity rather than superficiality, compassion rather than neglect and apathy for the sufferings and problems of others. One should be broad-minded rather than narrow- minded, detached rather than attached to the ego, self-content rather than prone to fall victim to temptations and to compromise. One should live with integrity and learn to forgive rather than hold grudges. One would have heard all these things. This is leadership.

However, unless one builds a strong and real foundation to build these values upon, one will not be able to withstand the temptations and the pressures of this world. We see all around us how people in elite positions, who could really have led the world in such incredible ways, have ruined their lives by just giving in to temptations. One little temptation and one's career, reputation and life is all ruined. There is a saying, "The bigger they are, the harder they fall." And the fact is, when one gets a position where one is affluent, the more people there are who want to destroy that person. Whether you are an industrial, social or spiritual leader, the bigger you are, the more you will have people who will envy you.

So, the question we are asking now is how to develop the real foundation of our true qualities that make us a real leader. This is not something that you will learn in the academic textbooks. You may learn what some of the qualities are and you may memorize them and you may try to practice them and apply them in your life, and that is very good. But if you build a magnificent mansion on sand, it will stand for some time, but when the storm comes, it will all fall, because there is no real foundation.

We should build our lives and qualities on a strong foundation: a foundation of real integrity, values and ethics based on truth. Then, no matter what comes in our life, we will not compromise. When the foundation of our values in life is in harmony with the laws of nature, we will live in harmony with our eternal nature. Now, how do we come to that point? Through spiritual practices, by which we experience and realize the truth, by which we have a philosophy, a science, to justify, to convince ourselves to carry on with patience rather than impatience, with compassion rather than apathy to other's sufferings, with integrity rather than compromising for some temporary gain, with forgiveness rather than grudge.

Forgiveness, Love and Leadership

When you have a grudge against someone or when you hate someone, if you introspect, you'll find that the whole experience is burning your heart; it's burning your consciousness; it's painful, it's contaminating. But as soon as you are able to forgive, you are liberated from that. Forgiveness is actually a beautiful, holistic experience for the heart. But how do we experience this? Unless we have a philosophy of life by which we understand what is the truth, who we are, and what is really, truly meaningful, fulfilling and worth striving for in our lives, what is really worth giving to others in our lives, it's difficult to experience it.

Sometimes we find that very popular leaders become cheaters, they become hypocrites. Why? Because their understanding is all theoretical, it is all academic. They know what's right, but they don't really have a higher philosophy and science based on actual truth to support it. So self-realization and enlightenment are the basis of a life of real prosperity. Such a life is a life of meaningfulness, of fulfillment; it's a life of love. If we don't learn how to love in our life, then everything else we do is empty and superficial. Because the heart wants love; the heart doesn't want money, the heart doesn't want beautiful women or handsome men. The heart is looking for love. But attaining that love is not a sentimental disposition; it's a science, it's a philosophy.

So, the most critical technique for proper living is to understand the nature of the self. Understand the nature of who we are; understand the nature of karma; understand how we do everything, how we speak, what we are responsible for. To understand the goal of life, of what we really want to strive for—that is the truth that should be the foundation of our lives.

PEACE–THE NEED OF THE DAY

Love Beyond Peace

Most people who meditate do so to find peace. That may be fine. The perfection of life, however, is not simply a neutral condition of peace but love. Love means the willingness to sacrifice oneself for the beloved. It is like the relationship of a mother with her child. Is the mother concerned with keeping peace in the house or is she concerned with taking nice care of the child? When a woman has a little baby, there is practically no peace in the house. The baby is crying all night long. The baby is responding to nature indiscriminately wherever it goes. The baby is looking for opportunities to break anything it gets its hands on.

The mother can easily give the baby to some baby-sitter saying, "You take care. I do not want to have anything to do with this." But the mother runs here and there, everywhere, trying to take care of the child. At times she stays up all night long. She worries about the child hurting itself. This is love.

Love is higher than peace, because in that love is eternal peace—not the peace of the mind, but the peace of the soul. Love means sacrifice—sacrifice even of our own peace for the pleasure of the beloved.

The Enemies Within

A few years ago, the whole world was discussing what took place on September 11, 2001, in New York City and in Washington D.C. and there was tremendous fear that such catastrophes may take place in other areas. There are people with intense egos who label themselves with religious designations to gather support and plunder innocent people on the basis of such faith.

God teaches us how to purify our heart. However, in the name of God, we see great cruelty and demoniac behavior. From where is this born? It's not just people that do the things; it's the envy in the heart, the hatred in the heart that drives them to do these things. We are taught to love the soul, but to hate the disease that is causing a person to forget the beauty of the soul. However many social reforms, however many prison houses we create, however many wars we declare, these catastrophes, these sufferings will keep coming as long as there is envy, pride, lust, anger, greed and illusion in people's hearts.

These internal misgivings are the enemies that are dropping bombs, creating concentration camps and torturing and murdering innocent people who have nothing whatsoever to do with war or threat; these are the enemies that are crashing planes into buildings, causing terror, fear, bloodshed, death and sorrow. So we should be compassionate and cultivate a feeling of sadness upon seeing others suffer and pray for them without discrimination. In fact, using our military, we can bomb and we can kill, and sometimes that is necessary for the protection of the citizens. However, unless we kill these enemies within our hearts, it will happen again and again.

Actually, the people responsible for these tragedies are really just like you and me; they have two arms, they have two eyes, they have a nose, they speak with their mouths, they walk with their feet, they hear with their ears, they have passions and desires, they are eternal pure spirit souls. However, somehow or other they are so much covered by these enemies, and their desires based on hatred, envy, pride and greed are so powerful that they are able to create such immense devastation. It is very sad. We not only feel compassion for the dead and the mourning, but we also pray for the souls of those causing such devastation. Real compassion is to pray in such a way that their souls can be freed from the shackles of these materialistic qualities so that they can actually live in harmony with nature.

War and Peace

Wars sometimes occur in this world. People do not know what peace is or how to achieve it. As long as there is no peace in people's heart, there will be war, there will be crime. There will be cruelty as long as we don't respect the soul: the souls of human beings, the souls of unborn humans, the souls of animals. If we do not live in harmony with nature and all the other living beings, then we are all actually creating a situation where individually and collectively there will be reactions. It's the law of nature.

The scriptures explain that the only enemy is the uncontrolled mind. It is the uncontrolled mind of people that performs such wicked acts. What is this fighting over a piece of land? It's actually ridiculous! Have you ever been to the Gaza strip or the Golden Heights that we keep hearing about? That's what people are fighting for. A piece of land—and a desert at that—is what has practically caused a world war. This is just one example, and there are many such examples in the world, of people fighting over some property, building nuclear bombs to kill each other for just a piece of property. And in a few years when we die, we will not even know that the property ever existed.

People who are so obsessed with thinking of destroying their neighboring states, are probably going to take birth in the neighboring state in their next life, because they are always thinking about them. And the bombs that they have created are going to cause their destruction in their next lives. That's the material world. Until we learn how to live in harmony with nature and all other living beings, we are always going to fight. That learning is only possible through purification because theoretical thinking may give us some direction, but realization is required to apply the theory.

Prayer for Universal Well Being

The highest prayer is the prayer to become a selfless instrument in God's hands. As Saint

Francis prayed, "Lord, make me an instrument of Your peace." He prayed not to receive, but to give; to be freed of all selfishness and to be filled with selflessness. He prayed to be the servant. He prayed to see that every living being is his master in the sense, "Let me be the humble servant to uplift, to help and to care for all my brothers and sisters in this world."

If you have boils on your body due to a blood disease, by putting some compress on the boils, you will get some temporary relief. But as long as the disease is in your blood, eventually there will be another boil and another and another. We have so many meetings—congressional meetings, United Nations meetings and altruistic meetings. They are trying to solve the problems of this world. Sometimes they can create some relief. But because there is still greed, pride, lust, envy, anger and illusion within the hearts of men, there is no question of peace. The disease remains.

Yes, we should also try to deal with the symptoms, but that's not enough. People are throwing waste into the rivers, the lakes, the oceans and the air. It's very good that we try to arrange some laws by which people don't dump these things into the oceans, the lakes and the sky. But that is not the solution because eventually they're going to dump it. What is the waste that they're dumping in the air, in the waters and on the earth? It is simply an expression of the dirt that is in their own hearts. They have created all these filthy, horrible things because they're motivated by greed.

Therefore, the only real solution is that there must be a change of heart. If we are not a part of the solution, we are a part of the problem. If our own heart is not being purified, then how will we help enlighten others? Therefore, we have to simultaneously deal with external realities of this world and try to make things better, but we must also know that the real solution is the purification of the heart, the unity of the soul with God. So the ultimate prayer is that we can be an instrument in the hands of God to bring about this unity and bring about this spiritual peace.

The Peace Prayer

What is the true nature of peace? Peace is not simply the absence of war. Peace must exist within us first, then, we can give it to others and create a world of peace.

We live in a time when our lives are disturbed, our environment is polluted, our relationships are distorted by an unnatural living pace. We feel apprehensive even in simple ordinary daily activities because of crime. Our bodies are sick due to unnatural elements in our food and in our environment. We do not know how to look within, how to see what is important, how to culture a natural balance.

There is a simple means to bring all things, within and without, into balance. It is the peace prayer. If we individually or collectively culture the practice of the peace prayer, then many things can be adjusted, within ourselves, and without, in our society.

What is the peace prayer? It is the singing of the Holy Names of God. In all religions and in all scriptures, it is part of our human heritage to chant the names of God. In different traditions, different names of God are used. There may be different types of instruments used, but the idea is still the same: to glorify the Supreme Lord by singing. If we join together and sing the Names of God, then there is a true possibility of world peace. As people of the world, we need to increase this practice—the result will come. At least, we ourselves will begin to know peace. At least, on a smaller scale there will be peace. All things will start to come into adjustment. If enough people participate in the peace prayer, we will bring the world into another era of spiritual cooperation, love, and purity. It will not take a large percentage; even a seemingly insignificant percentage is enough to tip the scales.

The peace prayer can be done in a number of ways. It can be done individually or collectively. It can be done formally or informally. It can be done at any time, and at any place. It can be done using any name of God found in any of the great religious traditions of the world. It can be done using any style of music. It can be done in a temple, a synagogue, a church, or a mosque. It can be done in any setting. Take this idea to heart and express it in your own special way. Share this idea with others.

The mantra we mainly use here is one from the Vedic tradition. The Vedas are the scriptures of India. This mantra is from the Kali Santarana Upanishad. It is:

Hare Krishna Hare Krishna
Krishna Krishna Hare Hare
Hare Rama Hare Rama
Rama Rama Hare Hare.

This mantra is known as the great mantra for deliverance. It is solely comprised of the names of God: Hare, Krishna, and Rama. This particular mantra has been given as the prayer for inner union with God through service. It means, "My dear Lord, please engage me in Your service."

YOGA AND MEDITATION

TUNING IN

The energy that is being transmitted by the antennas is everywhere. It is being transmitted through satellites; we can turn on a weather station, a news station, just by the touch of a button. We can turn on a soap opera or a drama where people are killing each other or a scene with romance or a religious channel; all we do is just press a button. What we are essentially doing is that we are accessing a particular frequency. There are unlimited frequencies everywhere in this world. By everything that we say, everything that we do, everything that we think, we are generating a particular energy and it goes right into the atmosphere all around us. It is very subtle, but it is very real. And which of these energies we are accessing is determined by the type of company we keep and by what we open our hearts and minds to. And that is why good company is important to feed our good qualities, to nourish our good qualities, to access the divinity within us and to access the divinity all around us.

In a business, intelligence is in proper investments. How you invest will determine your future. How much are people investing in the internal nourishment of their hearts today? How much are people investing in that which brings about peace and stability? Whatever we are and whatever we have is all that we can give to the society. A poor person can't give wealth to the society. If I am myself begging on the street, how can I help other beggars? Maybe I can help emotionally, but certainly not with food. So, what we have is what we can give. In this world today compassion is such a great need. In human life, it is really so essential to take responsibility because if we are not a part of the solution, we are a part of the problem.

Understanding Meditation

There are different forms of meditations in every religious tradition and practically in every denomination of each religious tradition. What is most important is our sincerity and the willingness to really absorb ourselves in that particular process. Some meditate on a silent mantra, some on a particular form, some on a particular prayer, some on a virtue, some on the breath, some on the different sensations of the body and some on the name of God, which is considered very divine and holy.

All these meditations are meant to purify our heart and bring our mind to its natural condition. Our consciousness is inherently pure, eternal, full of knowledge and bliss. But somehow or other it has been covered by and adulterated by so many misconceptions, so many desires, so many longings, so many anxieties about what we want and what we don't want "I am a man, I am a woman; I am American, I am South American, I am Indian, I am Pakistani, I am Russian, I am African"— all of these are bodily conceptions. We are so much consumed by these things and it is all mixed into our consciousness. If we filter our mind through meditation or any genuine spiritual practice, it brings our consciousness back to its original state, which is pure.

Another example is a mirror. When you look into a mirror, you see yourself. But what if that mirror has been neglected for hundreds of years? There are layers and layers of debris, dust, dirt and filth. And when you look into that mirror, all you see is the dust and the dirt that is accumulated, and all that you think is "This is me!" But when you clean the mirror, little by little you start seeing the image of yourself. And when the mirror is actually clean, you see who you are. Meditation is for that purpose; prayers are for that purpose; spirituality is for that purpose: to cleanse our heart, to cleanse our life-style so that we can actually directly experience our own essence, which is eternal, full of knowledge and full of love.

Yoga Means Unity

What is the meaning of yoga? Yoga means unity. What is the meaning of religion? Religion comes from the Greek word religio, which means "to bind back, to be in harmony, to be in unity." Every living being has a body, a mind and a consciousness. The consciousness is the energy emanating from the soul or the atma. So to harmonize the body, the mind and the soul is the art of yoga.

Yoga simply means to unite. To unite the body with nature is hatha–yoga. To create unity within the mind and the body is pranayama. To create unity within mind and the atma is jnana. To create unity between the soul and God is bhakti. That is the complete yoga system—unity. And in that unified condition, we can actually express the natural innate love, which we have found in our own life, in everything we do within this world.

All of us within our own hearts have unlimited tremendous spiritual power. The process of yoga, or the real, true process of religion, is not just to perform some rituals and have some social identity in which we protect ourselves from other people with a different religious or social identity. The essence of real religion or yoga is to access that incredible spiritual power and to express it in every aspect of our life. Then, with a pure heart, we can overcome many obstacles that seem impossible.

If we have unity, we can create unity. If our mind is in conflict, if our mind is not balanced with our body and with the needs of the soul, then there is a fundamental disunity in our life. When there are so many dysfunctional people who are not in harmony with their own consciousness, whose mind, body, and soul are not one in interest, in purpose, who are not unified, then there can be no real peace, there can be no real happiness, there can be no real love.

The Joy That Gives Birth to Eternal Joy

In the great religions of the world there are many processes or disciplines to help allow the light of love to shine from our hearts, to help purify our hearts from all of the unwanted qualities which are like the cloud covering the sun-like soul. According to the Srimad Bhagavatam the most highly recommended means of developing our love for God is vibrating the pure sound of God's Name. In each and every name of God, God has invested all of His power, all of His potencies. Simply by chanting God's Name, our hearts become purified. What you associate with, you become like. Therefore, try associating with spiritually-minded people, with saintly people. And by associating with God, we become saintly and we become godly.

Now, how do we associate with God? God is everywhere. God is within everything, but we are not conscious of His presence. Therefore, the Name of God is the manifestation of God in full, which can keep our consciousness constantly and always in connection with Him. It is such a simple and wonderful process. Whether one is a young man or a young woman, or an old man or an old woman, regardless of any of our qualifications or disqualifications, anyone can vibrate the Name of God. By that vibration we associate with the Supreme Truth, the Supreme Pure. Through that association we become purified.

Now, how do we chant the Name of the Supreme Lord? There are many ways. There are no hard and fast rules. But the essence is that our concentration should be attentively fixed on the pure sound of God's Name. So when we chant the maha-mantra Hare Krishna Hare Krishna Krishna Krishna Hare Hare / Hare Rama Hare Rama Rama Rama Hare Hare, we are not practicing a particular type of religious dogma. Every Name of God is universal. It is complete, but you have to chant some Name of God. It is not that any Name of God is limited to the boundaries of any type of sectarian dogma. We create labels which make it appear that way. The Name of God is perfect and complete. The Name of God contains the whole universe because God is appearing in His Name. Therefore, the most natural life is the life where we are always in contact and unity with God.

Everyone likes to dance. Everyone likes to sing. So sing and dance in the glorification of the Lord's Name. On every level we find joy, and that joy gives birth to eternal joy. The joys of this world have a beginning and an end, but the joys of glorifying the Supreme Truth awaken the eternal fulfillment of all of our desires.

When we chant and when we dance, whether we are chanting the name of Allah or Jehovah or Yahweh or Wakan–tanka, we are not concerned about which Name, provided it is a pure authorized sound. It's not that if you chant "apple, apple, apple", you will attain the same goal as if you chant the Name of God. The Name of God is revealed through His pure servants and through the scriptures of the world. If we simply accept a humble life in praise of God, then the light of the love of the soul within us will shine to give light to all creatures on earth. If we simply chant the Name of God, the Hare Krishna maha-mantra, we will find that great treasure of happiness, and we will have the ability to share that happiness with all.

Best Friend or Worst Enemy

Trying to practice yoga while engaging the mind in material enjoyment is like trying to ignite a fire while at the same time pouring water upon it. Yoga practice without mental control is of little or no value.

The mind can be controlled by engaging it constantly in the transcendental loving service of the Lord. When the mind is controlled it acts as our best friend. But it acts as our worst enemy when uncontrolled.

how to be successful ?

The Art of Work

The Gita teaches that the perfection of yoga is to perform our duty in divine consciousness. People often say that work is worship; the Gita (3.9) tells us what type of work is worship.

"Work done in devotion to God and in service to humanity liberates one from the bondage of material creation. On the other hand, work done for one's own selfish motives, without devotion and respect to God, is the cause of bondage."

The Bhagavad-Gita thus teaches us how to apply spiritual consciousness in our day-to-day life.

Arjuna and Duryodhana had the same occupation and were doing the same work: fighting. Yet Duryodhana is condemned and Arjuna is glorified. Why? Arjuna is glorified because, on hearing the Gita, he performed his duty selflessly. He did his work as an act of sacrifice: in divine consciousness and devotion to God, and for the upliftment of humanity.

Duryodhana did the same thing as Arjuna, but with no respect for the word of God. He did it for his own prestige, for his own power, to fulfill his own greed.

The primary teaching of the Gita is: how to change our consciousness.

No Pain, No Gain

To become humble, we have to struggle against the natural course of the way this world works and fight against our egoistic tendencies. And how do we do that? By accepting a subordinate position. It may be humiliating and torturous to our ego, but doesn't a champion weightlifter torture his muscles to make them strong? To be a proper athlete, doesn't it take tremendous effort and pain? To graduate from a prestigious university, doesn't it take a lot of effort and pain? The nature of the intelligence is to be ignorant. If a student just lets his intelligence do what it wants, he will remain ignorant. Because he is willing to go against that tendency of his intelligence, and struggle hard to study, to learn, to memorize, he succeeds. So, if we want to achieve anything worthwhile in life, we have to put our effort and be willing go through the pains needed to succeed.

The Foundation to Excel

Everyone seeks happiness. True happiness is a product of inner fulfillment. Through the ages, sincere people have turned to spiritual life in order to find a higher quality of life. The tendency in today's world is to be trapped in a life obsessed with quantitative rather than qualitative values. This tendency can imprison the mind in endless superficialities. Today, stress and anxieties are often daily realities, and even those who excel are often prisoners of their own success. The more we have, the more work it takes to sustain it, and the more people try to take it away from us. It's often like battling to swim upstream in the river of competition.

Real wisdom is to build our life on a strong foundation. This world we live in is a place of dualities and no one, whatever one's position may be, can escape from these dualities. There is success-failure, honor-dishonor, pleasure-pain, happiness-distress, victory-defeat, etc. If we build a strong internal foundation in life, then, whatever comes in our life—the ups, the downs, the rewards, the trials—we can grow from them, we can gain experience from them. We can deepen our love from any situation that comes upon us. We see the world according to our unique state of consciousness. A really successful person is one who sees a positive opportunity in every situation in life. Even in the darkest tragedies and traumas, there must be something to learn, some wisdom, some growth, some opportunity.

A diamond is nothing but an ordinary piece of coal, which with the help of nature's wisdom, has transformed into the most precious jewel under extreme pressure. Pressure can make us, pressure can break us. Tragedies can make us or they can break us. And even success, honor and glorification can make us or break us. To make a positive transformation takes a strong foundation. We should perform our duties with full power and determination and enthusiasm, and not be attached to the results of our duties. A happy, clear-thinking and fulfilling life requires that we learn the art of controlling the mind rather than being controlled by it. What greater need is there than the leaders of society, from all levels, to be exemplary in transforming greed into generosity, transforming envy into appreciation of others, transforming arrogance into humility, transforming our selfish passions into selfless love, service and compassion towards others, transforming despair into hope and seeing opportunities in whatever comes before us in life?

The Good and the Evil

The native American Indians have a way of explaining the internal conflict within all of us. They say that within the hearts or the minds of all of us are two dogs: a good dog and a bad dog. The bad dog is howling for vengeance, for immoral reckless action. And the good dog is calling out for morality, integrity, devotion. There is a battle between the two. The dog that we feed the most is going to be the stronger of the two. And how do we feed that dog? By the choices we make every minute, every day; by the values we hold sacred. Integrity means to feed the good dog, no matter how bad and loud the bad dog barks. This is the principle of every great scripture in the world.

Both good and evil are within all of us. And because they are within all of us, we have created them in the world around us. How to nourish our positive side, how to conquer greed with charity, hate with love, anger with forgiveness, apathy with compassion—these are essential questions. To nourish the positive and to starve the negative is the real advancement of civilization. If we have the determination and if we make the right choices to nourish our divine nature, we will be victorious in life.

Attitude Shapes Your Destination

The way we react to opportunities that come in life depends a lot on our attitude. In fact, the world is nothing but our vision covered by our attitude.

In the Mahabharata, the great teacher Dronacharya told his disciple Yudhisthira to go into the world and find one person who was worse than him. And at the same time he asked Duryodhana to go and find at least one person who was better than him. Both had learnt from the same teacher and both had become competent in their own ways. But the way they saw the world showed that they were in totally different frames of mind.

Yudhisthira came back and reported his findings. In

spite of carefully searching, he claimed that he could not find even one person worse than himself; everyone he met had some good quality which he himself did not possess. So his constant observation was of his own personal defects and others' good qualities. On the other hand, Duryodhana came back and claimed that he could not find even one person better than himself; he had tried his best, but he had realized that every person had at least one defect that he himself did not possess.

What determined their different conclusions and visions of the world around them? Their attitude, which was controlled by the culture in which they were raised, the kind of circle of influence they had around themselves, and the inner desires they nurtured.

Conflict Resolution

Conflict is the very nature of this material world. Even the cells within our bodies are in conflict.

The subtlest of all elements of creation is the false ego, and all other elements—earth, water, fire, air, ether, mind and intelligence—are both evolving from and resting upon the false ego. But what is the false ego? It is the false sense of identity.

"I am this body and all the designations of this body are mine. I am a man, I am a woman, I am black, I am an American, I am a Hindu, or I am rich." All of these are false identities connected with the body, which is constantly changing. When we were infant babies, we looked completely different; in our youth our bodies grew, and as adults we saw further change in our bodies. The Bhagavad-Gita says that we are not these temporary bodies; our true identity is that we are all eternal souls with a common origin, God. In every great religious scripture, God is described as the father and the mother. In the Bhagavad-Gita Lord Krishna says, "I am the seed-giving father of all living beings."

Unless human beings understand their common relationship with one another, with God in the center, there must be conflict—it is inevitable. My spiritual master, Srila Prabhupada, used to say that if we throw a stone in a pond it creates circles that expand to the end of the pond. If we throw more stones at the same place, all the circles will flow out harmoniously. But if we throw many stones in different parts of the pond, all of them will have their own different centers. Therefore, all the circles will collide. The water will become chaotic.

Conflicts on the basis of religion

God, the Absolute Truth, is unlimitedly variegated, but the false ego pollutes our consciousness and creates conflicts even based on the various understandings of the same God. If you are taught, "Two plus two is four," and I am taught, "Three plus one is four," we could declare war on each other on that basis; we could terrorize each other on that basis; we could create systematic education for our children to hate and to despise the heretics who think that four can be got through two plus two. But if we have higher knowledge, we can understand that they are both ways of approaching four. The false ego keeps our consciousness very small-minded, in an isolated condition. So it is no wonder that historically there has always been conflict in this world even based on religion.

Conflicts between Individuals and within one's own mind

Then there is conflict between individuals. Actually, the basis of all conflict is the conflict in a person's mind. For example, Hitler was a troubled, abused child. And he took it out on the world.

Let us examine the conflict within the mind. According to the World Health Organization the number three worst disease that causes suffering and death is mental illness. And within the next 30 years, it will be the number one disease causing pain, suffering and death in the world; worst than herpes or hepatitis C or cancer or heart disease. People's minds are disturbed. They are in conflict: conflict between good and evil, conflict between what should be done and what shouldn't be done.

How do we resolve conflicts?

Unless we spiritually clean our hearts of lust, envy, anger, greed, pride and illusion, there will be conflict within us and we will be tuned in to all the conflict around us. For example, when people become intoxicated, they get tuned in to all the negative vibrations that are floating around in the atmosphere, and they in turn become influenced in both subtle and gross ways by those vibrations.

Therefore, it is very important that we clean our hearts and simultaneously associate with people, activities and words that help us to tune in to those vibrations that will enlighten us rather than degrade us.

Failures as Stepping Stones to Success

My spiritual master used to say that it is a material principle that failure is the pillar of success, but it can also be applied to our spiritual lives. One very famous speaker has said, "Success is going from failure to failure to failure, without losing one's enthusiasm." We really never fail until we give up trying—trying with determination and enthusiasm. Vision means to see the invisible, to feel the intangible and to achieve the impossible.

Actually, challenges or failures can either be stepping stones or stumbling blocks on the road to success. It is all a matter of how we look at them. We can see a glass as half-empty, or we can see the same glass as half-full. One way of seeing will bring us enthusiasm, while the other way of seeing will bring us discouragement. We can apply that principle to every aspect of our life. But it is always important to be sure that we are doing the right thing.

We learn from our mistakes. A mistake is only a mistake if we fail to learn from it. Real leaders make many, many mistakes, but they do not repeat them. They learn from them, and they remain enthusiastic and determined for the goal. In every situation actual champions are always focused on their goals.

Failure builds character. Failure is something that only comes to one who earns it. We should respect failure as an honor. We cannot be successful unless we have the courage to fail. And every failure contains the seed of success. When we learn from mistakes, when we learn from failures, we become stronger, we develop greater integrity.

Thomas Edison tried 8000 various experiments before he finally invented the electric bulb. Later when he was asked about it, he said that he wasn't discouraged by all those 8000 failures. "From every failure I at least learnt what doesn't work." That attitude is success!

When difficulties, obstacles, pressures and even failures come into our lives, we should always be seeing the invisible, feeling the intangible, and in this way we can achieve the impossible. We may not understand the exact cause behind the difficulty, but if we have faith, if we have hope, we can always be looking at that "flower" that will grow from this "rainstorm." That attitude is the substance of a successful man. Opportunity knocks, but most people complain about the noise. We should see an opportunity in every situation; we never really lose until we stop trying. It is said that in the darkness a star shines the brightest.

A third-class man does not even begin to endeavor because he is fearful that he may fail. A second-class man endeavors, but turns back when faced with obstacles and failures on his path. But the first-class man keeps his mind fixed on the goal and does not turn back.

How to Achieve Self-Confidence?

Self-confidence is a very essential ingredient for success in any field of life. Without such confidence we are afraid to take risks; we also don't have the courage to explore higher horizons while performing our deeds within this world.

Real self-confidence is not based on our achievements or our successes in this world, but it is based on the realization of who we are, what our purpose is and what we represent to ourselves, to our families and to the world around us.

If a person has such self-confidence, then he can generate confidence and faith in others. Actually, to fail is not much of a loss; to lose one's character and integrity is a major loss to our inner life.

A person with proper disposition and attitude is willing to accept even major failures in the eyes of the world in order to preserve the high values that he or she believes in. If we're willing to sell our ideals, our ethics, our character, our integrity, and our very soul for the adoration of this world, then our so-called self-confidence will be built on a foundation of sand. It has no real substance and it can bring us no real fulfillment.

Six Common Indicators of Low Self-esteem

Low self-esteem really means a lack of real contentment within one's inner life.

1. People with low self-esteem like to gossip. Why? Because that's what gives them pleasure. They do not have any substance inside. On the other hand, people who are actually self-confident speak of their ideals in life and not of the faults of others.

2. A person with low self-esteem is quick to criticize others, whereas a person with some inner fulfillment is respectful to others and is naturally longing to show respect to others, to be caring toward others.

3. A person with low self-esteem is arrogant. He thinks, "I've done this, I've conquered these nations, I've made these millions, and I've won these tournaments and so on." Such people are very eager to try to convince other people of how great they are, how successful they are, and what they have accomplished within this world. But a person with actual self-confidence is humble. Why? Because he simply doesn't need to impress

people with cheap words of conceit. If you are actually very weak within, you have to brag about whatever great or little things you have done to try to get the approval, the recognition, and the adoration of others. But if you have inner contentment, if you have confidence in yourselves, you don't need that.

Once a sage in the Himalayas told me that when you do something good and you tell somebody about what you did, by that telling you exhaust most of the credits of what you have done.

4. In the world today we want to take credit for what we have not done and we want to give blame to others for what we have done. This is another quality of a person with low self-esteem. He makes excuses, and blames others for their apparent shortcomings, whereas a person with self-confidence doesn't make excuses, doesn't blame others, and takes responsibility for what he has done or what he has not done, and always strives to improve.

5. Persons with low self-esteem are dependent on the

appreciation, praise and approval of others, whereas persons with self-confidence are willing to speak what is true and do what is right even if it is very unpopular. Especially for the youth in the world today association is such a powerful influence. Most people smoke cigarettes, drink alcohol or do all illicit things, not simply because they really want to do it, but because they want to look cool and be accepted by the people around them. But integrity means we understand what is right and we do it—even if people criticize us, even if people make jokes or laugh at us. Eventually, those same people will come to us when they are in trouble because they understand that here is a person with integrity.

6. Those with low self-esteem are easily jealous about other people's successes. What is jealousy? That means we are so hollow, so empty within, there is so much lack of satisfaction about our worth, our value, and who we are, that we actually have to feel a type of hatred and jealousy towards others who appear to be better. A person with real self-confidence is the well-wisher of everyone. He is not so concerned with his reputation, but is

concerned with his character. He is not so concerned with what he can get and what he can prove to others by his fashion, by his way of speech, by his way of talk and by the type of furniture he has in his home. He is more concerned with what he is giving to others. Actual self-confidence doesn't mean we become absorbed in our egoistic self. The art of real self-confidence is to become selfless, because in becoming selfless there is inner fulfillment.

So it is very important to understand that real self-confidence is not simply about what we have achieved and what we have conquered, because that kind of self-confidence doesn't bring any real inner accomplishment: whatever we do, we always have to have more, more and more. Real self-confidence is when we're actually finding fulfillment and satisfaction with who we are and what we represent within this world. Some fools may think that, this type of self-confidence, this type of inner peace, is an impediment to making great strides of achievements in this world. However, the opposite is true. The purer our motives, the greater courage and faith we will have to accomplish things way beyond the horizon of even our imagination. When we have such inner self-confidence, anything we pursue is actually easy. It may be difficult mentally, and it may be difficult physically, but when we have the will, the confidence and the faith, that makes anything easy.

Unity is Strength

The topic of unity has been pondered, reflected, and pursued since time immemorial—how to create unity within this world? One of the greatest powers in all fields of life is unity.

But there is a fundamental problem: there are so many diversified distinctions between living beings. Everyone has their own conception of their identity, and this creates a natural conflict amongst those who look different, think different, or act different.

There has always been conflict between the castes, not only in India, but all over the world, though the castes may go by different names in different places. There is the educational class, there is the administrative class, there is the working class, and there is the class of trade and agriculture in every society. Also, there have always been distinctions and conflicts between nationalities, between races, between religions, between generations, between sexes, and between philosophers.

On practically every level of the world, there is reason for conflict. Even within a family, there's the older brother and the younger brother and that creates conflict. As long as everyone has their separate, independent interests, there will be conflicts.

There is an example: if you throw a stone in a clear pond of water, wherever that stone falls, it will create a circle, and that circle will expand, expand, and expand. If you put another stone and throw it into another part of that water, it will create another center, and from that center, the circle will get bigger and bigger. However many different places you put stones, there will be different circles, and they will all collide and create a tumultuous situation in the water. But if you throw every stone in the same place, because there is the same center, there is no conflict amongst the circles created.

On December 7, 1944, the Japanese bombed Pearl Harbor. Before that Churchill had been pleading with America to get involved in World War II because Hitler was conquering one nation after another. Since America was still reeling from a major depression, it was hesitant to enter the war. But when the bombs came to their own backyard, they realized, "We have to fight this. Whether we like it or not, we are in the world war. It's not a matter of choice; it's a matter of emergency." Because of the unity that resulted amongst the allied nations, they won the war. That is the strength of unity.

In India, one man, Mahatma Gandhi, unified the nation in such an incredible way. What could one little old man, who had taken a vow of ahimsa, nonviolence, do to the British Empire? At that time the British Empire was the most powerful force on earth, but this one small, old personality had the power to unify millions of people and that unity compelled the British Empire to give up.

Michael Jordan, one of the most popular and famous basketball players in the world, spoke something very interesting. He was in a game and there were just a few seconds left before the game ended. He was in a position from where he could easily throw the ball, and if he made that score, he would have established a world record in the history of basketball for making maximum points in a game. Everybody was so excited, but to everyone's great surprise, he passed the ball to one of his team mates who stood closer to the basket and that person made the point and they won the game. The newspapers asked him, "Why did you do that? You could have gone down in history." And he said, "I am not concerned with that. When I'm playing, I'm only concerned with the team. If you want a strong team, every team player has to think in terms of the team first and one's individual interests last; otherwise, the team cannot be a champion team." He continued, "Even though it was an easy shot for me, it was an easier shot for my teammate. So my passing the ball to him meant a greater chance of our team winning the game. That is more important than I going down in history." Because of this team spirit that team won almost every championship in that decade. That is the strength of unity.

Purpose of Knowledge

The conclusion as well as the goal of all knowledge is the complete cleansing of the mind and the heart of all material misgivings.

Theoretical knowledge that does not bring us to the point of becoming pure in heart is just like a heavy burden on our brain. It simply creates all sorts of false ego and a mumbo-jumbo of different ideas, concepts and philosophies, which are nothing but a burden. Therefore, to learn simply for the sake of accumulating knowledge is one of the greatest obstacles to spiritual advancement.

We have shining examples of great spiritual teachers who are conversant with so much knowledge of philosophy and so much realization. But all of that knowledge is simply targeted at cleansing the heart to become the humble servant of the Lord. Knowledge is like a seed and our heart is like an agricultural field. Unless the heart is properly ploughed and made receptive to receive the seed, the seed will simply be lost.

Publishers Note

We would like to express our sincerest thanks to Mr. Suresh Sawant who has so kindly conceptualized and created the cover page for this book. We would also like to thank Hemangi Oza, Suchitra Prabhudesai, their efforts have been extremely selfless and worth appreciating. We thank all the volunteers who have helped in transcribing the talks by Radhanath Swami.